AFRICA'S
New COAT

Written by
CLIFF FAULDER

cliff.faulder@aboutfacetraining.co.uk
https://aboutfacetraining.co.uk/

Printed in England
First Edition Published in 2022 by AboutFace Publishing

ISBN 978-1-7399283-1-5 (ANC Hardback)
ISBN 978-1-7399283-0-8 (ANC Paperback)
ISBN 978-1-7399283-2-2(ANC E-Book)

Summary: A children's book that explores difficult conversations
about fairness, right and wrong and friendship.
1. Children—Education —Friendship.
2. Brave Conversations
3. Relationships—Anti Racism—Anti Bullying—History—Culture

To the loves of my life. My wife Maxine and my children Rahiem, Jahrome, Romeo and Zahne. My sisters Elicia and Rema and all the brave souls who refuse to give up on the dream of a king and a race without fear.

"**A**fricaaaaaaaa! Africaaaaaaaa!" called Africa's mother from the bottom of the staircase.

Africa sat on the edge of her bed, grinning ear to ear with both hands clasped over her mouth to muffle her shrieks and giggles. "Africaaaa! It's already 8 o'clock, and I can't believe you would not be up and dressed by now. Have you forgotten what a special day it is?" Africa could hear her mother beginning to walk upstairs muttering, "I cannot believe this, when I was a little girl, I was ready for school before it was time to go to bed."

Africa's heart raced with excitement as she wriggled with glee waiting for her mother to enter her bedroom. Africa was all too aware of what a special day it was today. She had spent months asking her mother when she would be able to have the wonderful coat that she had seen her mother wearing in photographs when she was a child herself. She knew where it was, but had never ever seen it up close; it was kept in a locked trunk in her mother and father's bedroom. Last year she thought she had caught a glimpse of it as her mother was putting it back into the heavy wooden trunk that sat under the bedroom window.

"What are you doing mother?" she had said from the bedroom doorway. "Was that the coat you are wearing in the picture of you and grandmother in the garden when you were small like me?" Africa's mother smiled without looking up. "Yes my love, it is" she said. Her eyes glazed were full of sparkle.

"Can I see it? Can I wear it? Wait!... Can I have it?" Africa's feet danced as she flapped her hands excitedly.

Africa's mother paused for a moment and then spoke softly as she often did when she wanted Africa to really hear what she was saying. "Africa. Come in and sit with me a while."

As Africa entered the room her mother closed the lip of the trunk and locked it with the small key that hung on a beautiful beaded necklace fastened around her elegant long neck. As Africa sat next to her mother, her mother placed a hand on Africa's knee. "Africa, what do you know about the coat I keep in the trunk?" Africa answered without thinking and quickly bleated out, "It's pretty." "And?" Africa's mother said hopefully, raising her eyebrows and tilting her head while she waited for a better answer.

7

"It's big" blurted Africa once more. As the words left Africa's mouth, she knew that this did not seem to be the answer that her mother was looking for. "My dear sweet child" said Africa's mother, moving her hand to the top of Africa's curly afro hair that sat proudly on top of her little head. "My dear sweet, beautiful little girl. One day you will wear that coat, but that day is not today. That coat is a wonderful gift that you will wear like so many princesses and queens before you. But at this time, you are not yet ready to understand the true value of the coat. But one day you will."

Africa giggled as she thought of that moment in her mother's bedroom. Was it really a year ago? I was so small then, she thought. Just then Africa's mother flung the door open with a stern look on her face expecting to see Africa fast asleep and still in her pyjamas. Africa couldn't hold back any longer as she leapt to her feet with her arms spread out wide laughing at the trick she had played on her mother as her feet danced once more, spinning, and twirling to show how ready for school she was. "Africa! That is not funny" her mother said while laughing and tickling her. "Are you ready?" She finally said as they stopped for a moment. "Yes mother, I am ready. I know now that the gift you are giving me today means a lot to you, and if you love it and have taken care of it, I must love it and take care of it too. Africa's mother smiled and nodded with slightest of nods.

"Ok. Well let's go and get your coat." As her mother took the key from around her neck, the world seemed to be moving in slow motion. Africa stared at the lock on the trunk as the key entered and turned. The hinges creaked and let out a high pitched squeak that you would expect to hear when opening a pirate's treasure chest.

And then suddenly there it was.

Africa's new coat.

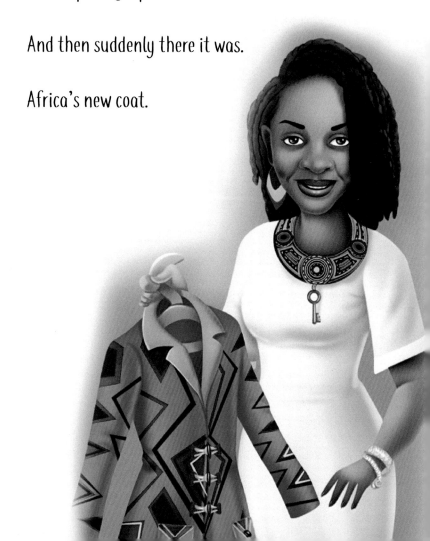

As her mother helped her slip her arms into the sleeves and the fabric slid over her trembling hands, she felt different.

Africa arrived at school wearing her beautiful coat.

Although it was new to Africa, the truth is it wasn't new at all. It had been in her family for a very long time. Africa's mother had worn it, her grandmother had worn it; in fact many people in Africa's family had worn it. Africa loved her coat. It was long and it was comfortable. Africa's coat had different colours and textures, as well as deep pockets that she could keep all types of wonderful things in that made her feel good.

Every day Africa wore her coat and it protected her from ever feeling unsafe or cold. It was like wearing a hug from somebody who loved you very much indeed.

One day, while Africa was playing by herself in the school playground, she noticed two children she had not played with before. Africa and the two children smiled at each other and, before long, they were talking on the playground.

"My name's Africa. What's your name?" speaking to the taller, older looking boy.

"My name's George," said the boy, "George Blighty, and this is my little sister Rose."

Rose smiled and said, "Hello Africa."

Before long, the children were playing together and having quite a lot of fun. Africa noticed that George would often stop playing for a moment to check on his little sister Rose. "Rose, are you ok?" He would say, and Rose would answer "I'm ok George, but I am a little bit cold." Again, they would play and for a while everything was fine, until George would stop and once again ask Rose if she was ok, and each time Rose would say "yes George I'm ok, but I am still a bit cold."

Eventually, George stopped playing and turned to Africa and said "Africa, can you help me and my sister?"

Africa replied, "I'll try, what seems to be the problem?"

"Well," George said. "My sister is not enjoying playtime as much as you and I." Africa looked at Rose, and Rose indeed looked sad. George spoke again "Africa, I think that I have a great idea to stop her feeling sad."

"Really" said Africa. "That's great! What can we do to help Rose?"

"Africa," said George, "it would really help if Rose could wear your coat!" Africa was a little bit surprised. "My coat?"

"Yes, your coat" repeated George. "You see. .,
it would make her ever so happy, and you don't
want people on the playground to think you are
selfish, do you?"

After thinking about it for a short while, Africa
began to undo the shiny black toggles that
fastened the front of her beautiful coat.

Africa paused on the second toggle. "But George,"
Africa said as she fumbled nervously with the
fancy button between her fingers. "But George,
I'm not sure my mother would be ok with me
letting someone wear my coat, and besides it
looks like the sun may well break through the
clouds any moment."

George interrupted Africa. "Now see here Africa! I don't know what your mother and father teach you in your household, but I'm quite sure you will find that in the house of Blighty we jolly well know the value of sharing!"

George stood in front of Africa. His brow furrowed but his mouth attempted to force a smile that seemed quite estranged to the look in his eyes.

"Africa, it would be the right and proper thing to do" he said.

"Unless..."

George paused, as he quickly glanced over his left and right shoulders, as if he had a message that was for Africa's ears only. Lowering his voice to a whisper, the half smiling George continued.

"Unless...your family simply does not understand the rules that are part of everyday good manners. Maybe you just don't know how to behave like the rest of us?"

Africa's heart sank. "Is that really what people would think of me George?"

"I'm afraid so," asserted George, whose face had softened somewhat.

"Well, it's not true! My mother and father have always encouraged me to be kind to other children." Africa uttered, as she hurriedly unfastened the remaining toggles.

No sooner was the last clasp free that George hastily stripped the fabric from Africa's shoulders and roughly peeled the coat from her arms. Without a word of thanks, George strode away from Africa as she trailed in his wake.

"Here you are Rose!" proclaimed the now boastful George, as he presented the precious gift to Rose. "Just like I told you, trust me and I will make sure you want for nothing."

George stood behind Rose and draped the coat across her back. As Rose lifted her arms through the sleeves and felt the silk lining brush against her skin, she stared at Africa and smiled. Africa smiled back, as she knew only too well the pleasure her coat was giving to her new friend. She watched as Rose skipped and danced, spun and twirled so hard that the hem of the coat floated up as the wind rushed beneath it. Africa smiled in George's direction, but he had adjusted his position slightly and she could only see the back of his head as he watched his sister frolic in the coat, he had provided for her.

"Do you think Rose is warm enough now?" enquired Africa but George did not answer.

Rose loved the coat and wore it proudly; she enjoyed the many compliments she received from others in the playground. "Wow!" exclaimed one child. "Is that new?" started another. "Where did your mother buy it from?" began a third. Africa took a deep breath and stepped forward, as she prepared to take her cue from Rose who would surely redirect the adoring few to her, as the rightful owner of the coat. "It is rather smashing, isn't it?" Rose stated coyly. "It's one of a kind you know. It's mine and I deserve it."

At that very moment, Africa realised that the coat wasn't being borrowed - it had been stolen!

"Excuse me," said Africa, in a bit of a panic, as she attempted to push past George "I need to have a quiet word with Rose."

Without warning, George thrust out an arm blocking Africa's way, as she fought her way through the ever-growing number of Rose's new friends. George's tone was very different now. His voice was cold and emotionless.

"Africa, it's Impossible to have my sister's coat."

"Your sister's coat!" A wide-eyed Africa said in disbelief.

"Why yes." George replied without missing a beat. "Rose has become accustomed to being warm and has many friends because of her new coat and that, my dear, is how it shall stay."

Africa began to shiver and become cold as she stood on the playground. She stared at the ground and wrapped her arms around herself to try and keep warm. As she did so, she began to feel ill, but could not decide if it was due to the cold or her sadness because she no longer had her coat.

She was all alone.

Looking from across the playground, Rose felt sorry for Africa. Not enough to give the coat back, but just enough to ask George to help her organise a whip round on the playground to see if they could raise enough money to make Africa not feel bad about having her coat stolen.

George gathered some of the playground's most popular boys and girls and offered them the opportunity to touch, feel or even try the coat on, if they would donate a small fraction of their own lunch money to the charitable cause if they would take pity

on the increasingly shabby and sickly-looking child that Africa had become. Most of the children tutted loudly and simply walked away. After all, this was not their problem. In fact, many of them sneered that if Africa was meant to have a fine coat, then she would have had one when she arrived at school.

Che, one of the children from a less popular group, overheard what was being said about Africa and decided to speak up. "Actually, I saw Africa this morning and she did have a coat. As a matter of fact, the coat that Rose is wearing is Africa's coat." One of the popular boys butted in; "Be that as it may, Africa is not in possession of the coat now. And what's more, if she was foolish

enough to lose it then she ought not to have had it in the first place. "

"Hear! Hear!" those that stood around George mumbled.

Che was disappointed with the other boys and girls and could not believe that they would not join him in getting Africa's coat back. Still, he went and stood with Africa and comforted her.

At the end of the day, £12 had been raised for Africa. Every person who had chipped in felt very proud of all that they had done to help Africa. £12 was not nearly enough to buy Africa a coat, but enough to make Rose feel less guilty for taking Africa's coat. George felt it was too much, so he kept £5 of the £12, after all, he helped collect it. Africa took the £7 in loose change from George and stared at it. Africa realised it couldn't buy her a coat, but it was enough to buy her a scarf that would keep some of the cold out and stop her coughing as much.

At the end of the school day, as she trudged home, Africa thought about her coat and remembered how wonderful it had made her feel. She remembered the warmth and the way the fabric felt against her skin. As Africa walked, she shuddered with shame as she thought about what her mother and father would say when she arrived home without her coat. Once again, the tears began to fall from Africa's eyes as she made her way - step by step - along the garden path and into the house where her mother sat in her armchair reading. Africa's mother looked up from her book and saw her daughter crying.

"Africa! Whatever is the matter? What has happened?"

Africa's mother knelt down and wrapped her arms around Africa, who was now sobbing so much she wasn't able to find the words in order to explain what had happened. Africa's mother called out for Africa's father, who came rushing to see what had happened. For the next few minutes, Africa, her mother and her father all sat in a circle, while Africa explained what a rotten day she'd had. Africa's parents wiped her tears and held her closely as the sun began to set. The sun began to hide, as if to signal it was time to let go of a day filled with sorrow.

"My dear, beautiful Africa" said Africa's mother in her soft loving voice. "I understand why you are upset, but I need to tell you something. It is the most wonderful secret, and it is found amidst the world's most beautiful truths."

Immediately, Africa stopped sniffling and slowly pulled back from her mother and father's embrace so that she could see their faces.

"What is it mother? Please tell me what it is," she replied. "Please tell me the beautiful truth so that it can take away the pain and sorrow I feel, now that my coat has been stolen."

Africa's mother and father looked at her and paused, until they were sure she had stopped speaking and they were certain that they had her full attention. With gentle hands, they reached out to Africa, each of them taking her by the hand once more, as they leaned in, as though to kiss her on the cheek like they did every night before bed. Africa felt like her heart would explode as she drew in a large breath of air, causing her to gasp! And then they spoke. The words leaving their mouths at the exact same time, spoken with love and joy and sunshine.

"Africa. The coat is a wonderful thing and indeed it is special. But it is nothing without the love inside the person who wears it. What makes the coat beautiful, my dear sweet Africa, is you. It is you who are the world's most beautiful prize."

Just then there was a knock on the front door. As Africa and her mother remained on the floor still holding hands, Africa's father got up to see who was at the door. Africa smiled at her mother and her mother smiled back. Africa felt much better.

Then suddenly Africa's fathers voice filled the air: "Africa! Africa!" her father called.

Africa went to the door to see what her father needed, and to her surprise there stood in the doorway was Rose clutching Africa's coat in her hands. "Rose!" Africa blurted out.

Before Africa could say another word, Rose thrusted the coat into Africa's hands.

"I'm so very sorry Africa." said Rose as she began to sob. "I really am sorry for taking your coat." Africa stood still in the doorway, one hand on her coat the other holding onto her father.

Inside, Africa felt angry, as she thought about all the pain Rose and her brother, who was nowhere to be seen now, had caused her. Africa thought about the way she had been cheated out of her coat and how she had been treated when she was left cold on the playground. Africa gripped her father's hand even tighter. She was angry. She wanted Rose to feel just as hurt as she had felt when Rose had taken from her and left her feeling hurt.

Rose spoke again. "I understand that you are angry, and you have the right to be. I really am sorry, I wouldn't blame you if you never spoke to me again."

Africa wanted to say angry words, but as she looked at Rose, she felt something else other than anger. The words of her mother and father still ringing in her ears. The beautiful truth is that the beauty of the coat was the wearer, not in the coat itself.

Africa decided to have a brave conversation with Rose. It took all her courage, but Africa wanted to understand why Rose had acted the way she acted.

"Why did you take my coat Rose?" asked Africa. "Why?"

Rose looked so sad, but grateful that she and Rose could talk about what had happened that day with the coat and their friendship.

"In all honesty Africa, I am not really sure why I took your coat. At first, I just really liked it. I liked how you looked in it and I saw how happy the coat made you. I just wanted to have the same feeling."

"But you knew the coat was mine Rose and when I asked for it back, both you and George told everyone it was yours," continued Africa. "You didn't seem to care how it made me feel. Why?" Africa repeated.

"I really wasn't thinking," she replied. "George was so sure that you didn't really need the coat as much as I did. Then, when everybody started to tell me how nice I looked, I just felt like I couldn't help wanting to feel that way for as long as I could."

Africa stood opposite Rose, her eyes fixed on every one of Rose's facial expressions, watching, as the little girl in front of her searched for the right words to explain what had happened.

Rose paused, while shaking her head open mouthed, "I really can't explain it Africa. I just felt like I deserved it more. George made me feel like the coat was mine."

Africa frowned. "And I didn't deserve the coat?" she said, barely above a whisper.

Rose stared back at Africa, but this time she had no words. Africa sat down on her doorstep and motioned for Rose to join her by patting the space next to her as she shuffled to one side. Rose half smiled with relief and was soon sat beside Africa.

"Rose" Africa said. "I am going to say something to you and I want you to listen carefully without interrupting. Some of the things I will say might be difficult for you to accept at first, and it may even make you feel uncomfortable, but I want you to understand that this is said out of love. I hope that it will help you, if you should ever find yourself tempted to behave like this in the future. I need you to be brave. Can you be brave, Rose?"

Rose looked directly at Africa and took a deep breath. "Yes, I can be brave" Rose replied confidently.

"Rose, you have already apologised for taking my coat and lying and I thank you for returning it to me. I can see that you are sorry and that you did not like the way that wearing a coat that wasn't yours to wear made you feel. But I can't help feeling that you are not quite sure why you acted that way, and if we don't think about that, then there is a chance that it might happen again? Does that make sense Rose?"

Rose nodded. "I think the reason that you and your brother took my coat was that you have never known what it feels like to not be in the position of privilege. Maybe you have been taught to feel this way by people you know, love and trust. I think that you and George took my coat because you have become used to getting whatever you want; whenever you want it.

The world we live in is also responsible for you and George feeling and acting the way you did, because that is the message we all see on television, in books and on billboards. Therefore, if you see something that you like, you now expect to have it, regardless of whom it belongs to and how they may feel if you take it from them; It is a very privileged position to be in, Rose.

I am not telling you off, I do not believe that this is your fault, it is probably the result of behaviours that you have seen, beliefs that you have heard and lessons that you have been taught. The thing is, that way of thinking and acting causes hurt and suffering for someone else."

Africa's voice cracked as she held back tears and tried to swallow the lump in her throat. "Just as I was hurt, upset and cold when you took my coat" she continued. "So, you see Rose, it is very important, in future, not only to think about how your actions may make someone feel, but also observe and listen when they speak about how you and maybe others have made them feel. This is not always easy and doing the right things will not always make you popular, you might even fall out with George, but the feeling you get when you do right by others is what life is all about. That feeling!"

Africa paused as her mind raced in a frenzy to find the right words. "That very feeling is the magic you felt when you and George saw me wearing the coat. Rose" Africa continued. "The coat is beautiful it's the love that shines out of a person's heart that makes the difference. It bubbles up from inside you and it makes everyone around you feel good too. Just like when you, George and I first started playing. Think about how good it felt just to be us in that moment."

Rose smiled the faintest of smiles and the more she remembered the more her smile grew.

"Once you understand, hopefully you wouldn't want to do something like that again." Africa smiled a rueful smile and put an arm around Rose.

They hugged. The type of hug that means something. The type of hug that means everything. The type of hug that makes you feel like you're wearing a special coat, woven out of love.

And they were alright.

ABOUT THE AUTHOR

Cliff Faulder's life has been as eventful as it has been fun. Born in Birmingham, England, to his parents Tom and El Freda, Cliff grew up listening to wonderful stories about his parents' childhood in Jamaica.

He was inspired to create stories off the top of his head to entertain his friends in school. Throughout his school years at Fairfax secondary School in Sutton Coldfield, Cliff was happiest when he talked with people. He was often the only person of colour in this environment. He developed and built genuine human connections with various people regardless of where they were from, thus challenging stereotypes and prejudice wherever he went.

After leaving school, Cliff used his love of talking to people to embark upon various careers, from salesman to rap artist. Later, becoming a senior director for many of Birmingham's top therapeutic childcare services. Working closely with children who faced many emotional and physical challenges, Cliff once again found his ability to create stories helpful to the children in his care and the adults who supported them.

Although Cliff no longer works directly within therapeutic children's services, he still helps countless children and adults develop greater human connections through his anti-racism training organisation AboutFace Training ltd. At AboutFace, Cliff continues to share stories such as Africa's New Coat to do what he does best…
Bring people together.